*For my husband, Frank, who is happiest on a snowy day
and instilled that love in our children.*
—N.H.

To each of you, whose heart belongs in more than one country.
—G.G.

———————————————————

Library and Archives Canada Cataloguing in Publication

Title: Snow doves / Nancy Hartry ; [illustrated by] Gabrielle Grimard.
Names: Hartry, Nancy, author. | Grimard, Gabrielle, illustrator.
Identifiers: Canadiana 20200209418 | ISBN 9781772601350 (hardcover)
Subjects: LCSH: Stories without words.
Classification: LCC PS8565.A673 S66 2020 | DDC jC813/.54—dc23

Printed and bound in China

*Second Story Press gratefully acknowledges the support of the Ontario Arts Council
and the Canada Council for the Arts for our publishing program. We acknowledge the
financial support of the Government of Canada through the Canada Book Fund.*

ONTARIO ARTS COUNCIL
CONSEIL DES ARTS DE L'ONTARIO
an Ontario government agency
un organisme du gouvernement de l'Ontario

Canada Council
for the Arts

Conseil des Arts
du Canada

Funded by the Government of Canada
Financé par le gouvernement du Canada

Canadä

Published by
Second Story Press
20 Maud Street, Suite 401
Toronto, Ontario, Canada
M5V 2M5
www.secondstorypress.ca

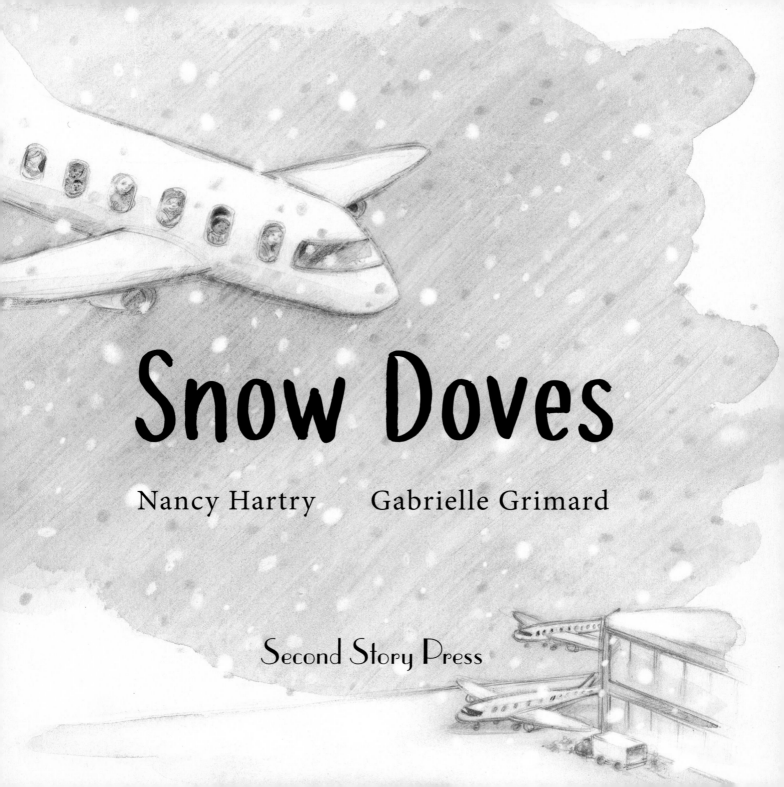

Snow Doves

Nancy Hartry   Gabrielle Grimard

Second Story Press

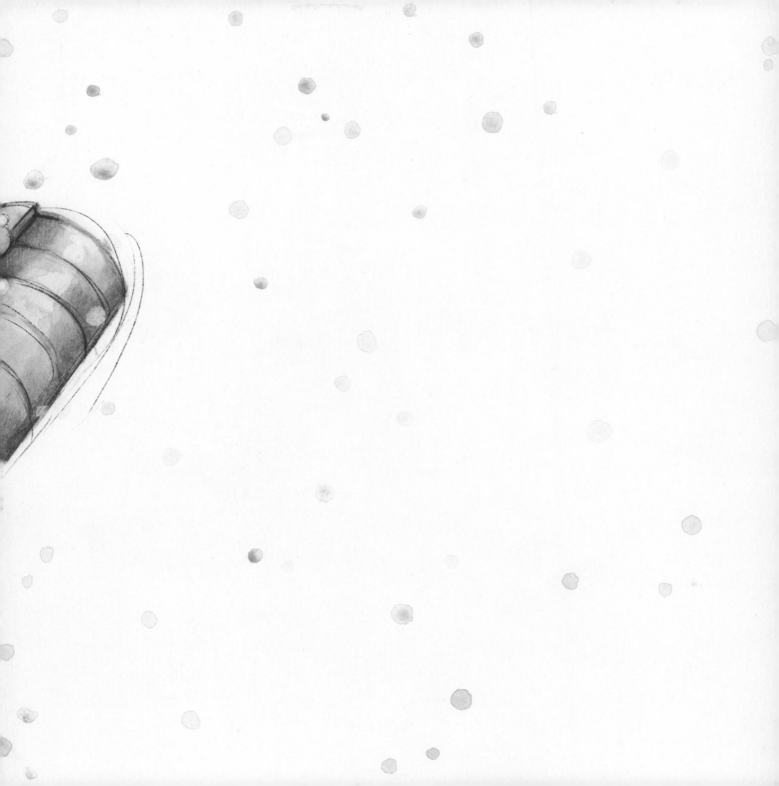

About the Author
NANCY HARTRY is the author of the successful picture book *Jocelyn and the Ballerina* and the YA novel *Smokescreen*. Her novel *Watching Jimmy* won the Canadian Library Association's Book of the Year for Children Award. Nancy lives in Toronto.

About the Illustrator
GABRIELLE GRIMARD has illustrated dozens of picture books, including *Stolen Words*, *The Magic Boat*, and *Lila and the Crow*. She lives in Quebec with her two children, several chickens, and her husband, who builds wooden boats.